I0624662

1

And the Evening and the Morning Were the Seventh Day

A Play About Different Times Occurring in One Place, in "Our Park"

by Lowery Christopher Collins

And the Evening and the Morning Were the Seventh Day

A Play About Different Times Occurring in One Place,
in "Our Park"

by Lowery Christopher Collins

NOTICE

COPYRIGHT

CAUTION: Professionals and amateurs are hereby warned that performance of AND THE EVENING AND THE MORNING WERE THE SEVENTH DAY is subject to payment of a royalty and that all rights to this work are controlled exclusively by LOWERY CHRISTOPHER COLLINS, without whose permission in writing, no performance of it may be given. It is fully protected under the copyright laws of the United States of America and of all countries covered by the International Copyright Union and all countries with which the United States has reciprocal copyright relations. All rights, including amateur/stage rights, motion picture, recitation, lecturing, public reading, radio broadcasting, television, video and/or sound recording, Internet, and all other forms of mechanical or electronic reproduction, such as CD-ROM, CD-I, DVD, electronic or cloud storage, information storage and retrieval systems and photocopying, and the rights of translation into foreign languages, are strictly reserved.

Conscientious observance of copyright law is not only ethical, but it also encourages authors to continue creative work. No alterations, deletions, or substitutions may be may made in the work without the prior written consent of the author or his legal representative.

ROYALTIES and INQUIRIES

Royalty must be paid every time this play is performed whether or not it is presented for profit and whether or not admission is charged. A play is "performed" anytime it is acted before an audience.

All inquiries concerning any performance rights should be addressed to the playwright: L. Christopher Collins, P.O. Box 223, Carthage, Texas 75633 or mrchriscollins@hotmail.com.   Website: www.christophercollinsonline.com

CREDIT and ADVERTISEMENT

Anyone receiving permission to produce AND THE EVENING AND THE MORNING WERE THE SEVENTH DAY is required to give credit to the author as sole and exclusive author of the play on the title page of all programs distributed in connection with performances of the play and in all instances in which the title of the play appears for purposes of advertising, publicizing, or otherwise exploiting the play and/or a production thereof. The name of the author must appear on a separate line in which on other name appears, immediately beneath the title and in size and type equal to 50% of the size of the largest, most prominent letter used for the title of the play. No person, firm, or entity may receive credit larger or more prominent than that accorded the author.

AND THE EVENING AND THE MORNING WERE THE SEVENTH DAY,
A PLAY ABOUT DIFFERENT TIMES OCCURRING IN ONE PLACE,
IN "OUR PARK"

Written by Lowery Christopher Collins

Copyright © 2020 by Lowery Christopher Collins

All rights reserved. No part of this book may be used or reproduced in any manner
whatsoever without written permission except in the case of brief quotations
embodied in critical articles and reviews. Printed in the United States of America.
For information, contact Ponderlake Publishing, P.O. Box 223, Carthage, Texas
75633.

Ponderlake Publishing: www.ponderlake.com

Playwright and/or Royalty Information: www.ChristopherCollinsOnline.com

ISBN 978-1-7349926-5-6

Ponderlake
Publishing

And the Evening and the Morning Were the Seventh Day

BY LOWERY CHRISTOPHER COLLINS

Cast of Characters

<u>MALES</u>

Arnold
Jim
Walter
Andrew
Spade
Vince
Rich
Steve
George

<u>FEMALES</u>

Elizabeth
Alice
Mary
Gloria
Stella
Nicole
Joan
Lisa

And the Evening and the Morning Were the Seventh Day

By Lowery Christopher Collins

Setting: *A park in the city. There is a concrete park bench and several trees around. However, one tree is dominant. In addition, there is a heavy-duty wrought-iron fence to the left of the bench.*

For the first segment, time is suspended. It does not exist at this point.
***ARNOLD**, dressed in denim overalls walks out on stage. He has already lived seventy years and has died; however, in his current existence, he appears to be about thirty. He walks confidently, yet hesitantly. He addresses the audience directly.*

ARNOLD: Well. Pauses. What a way to begin this conversation, if you will. The word well. (*Shakes his head*) I was born about 3 miles over there in 1893. Points. And I was buried about 3 miles over there in 1963. (*Points in the opposite direction.*) That was a good amount of time—not nearly as much as I would have wanted, but I can't complain. I won't complain. Seventy years is a decent life. Three score and ten, you know. A lot happened between 1893 and 1963. Wars, modernization, the car, the airplane, for land's sake. And my life. Marriage, kids, grandkids, a whole passel of people you helped make with the fruit of your loins. It's good to have 'em. People who love you. People you live for. I wouldn't give up the memories at all. I've witnessed more and . . . well, I am rambling. 1893 to 1963. Not bad. Not bad at all. And what was in between that place I came kicking and screaming into this world and that place where I lay down and left it? Why, everything! Everything I ever knew. Everything I ever loved . . . and hated . . .and didn't care either way about. I lived in the same house for the last forty years of my life, and I lived with the woman I loved. Pure, sweet, good wife. Better mother. Excellent friend. That's what counts most, isn't it? Someone who'll stick it out with you. Love you through your faults and hers? To work with you and for you and in spite of you. And when it's all said and done, you leave them anyway…? When I was a kid, we farmed. Hard work: farming. Has a way of roughing up the hands. Also has a way of making them stronger. We lived just on the outskirts of this town. Close to the general store. Closer to the fields. When I married Grace, we moved into town, this very town. It was a good place to raise a family. Yeah, I missed sowing and reaping crops, but I had a good job. And I wasn't far from the old home place. And come to think about it, it wasn't far from my final home place. Life centered here. This town. Come to think of it, this park. Look at this place. Right in the center of town. The first settlers to this place used to gather here, I guess because it's just about the most peaceful place in these parts. It's been the town park for as long as I can remember. It's a peaceful place. Mostly. For years, people have come here to think or talk to do a variety of other things. Back in 1917, we meet here to talk of war. I remember it like it yesterday. In '29, Hiriam Mobar hung himself from that very tree. He wasn't quite as happy in his money—or lack of it as we all thought. Same with that Mr. Corey. Many a couple have shared a kiss or more...or even a marriage proposal in this very place. In '57, Bonnie Durham gave birth to twins right over there....couldn't get to the doctor in time. Legend has it that Nancy Bouchaine killed her husband, Grey, on this very spot before she disappeared. It was not a pretty sight. I even had quite a few happy moments here myself. This park is a pretty amazing little place. You are probably going to see moments that have occurred here. Different people, different times unaware of each other. And time is a friend, not an enemy...keep in mind. Not all things happen in the order you're used to. It's amazing how something small from 1925 could have such an impact on something what happened to me twenty years later. I'm sure you can something about that with your life. Ever think about something that happened ten years ago and something that happened ten months ago together? So, if you see Stella and Alice, or Ally, and Walter and Nicole and yes, Jim, *(he pauses)* keep that in mind. I think a lot now . . . and I go from 1930 to 1948 back to 1905. And your time. A wise man once wrote in a poem, "It takes life to love life." There's a lot to love. How true.

Time now becomes real, yet disjointed.

It is 1967. A young woman, **ELIZABETH***, 18, walks onto the scene. She is wearing a bright yellow, sequined prom dress. Beaming from ear to ear, she looks all around in awe. Before speaking, she twirls around one full rotation.*

ELIZABETH: My! Oh, my! I've never seen this place look so beautiful. Jim! Jim! Come on. Look at the park tonight.

JIM, 18, enters from stage right. He is wearing a snow-white tuxedo. His bow tie and vest are a shiny yellow in color.

ELIZABETH: Jimmy, beau of mine, just take a look at the park tonight. I don't think I've ever seen it look so romantic.

JIM: Romantic. Romantic? Is that what you call it?

14

ELIZABETH: Of course, Jimmy. The moonlight on the trees. The reflection of the pond. The silhouetted bench and railing. Everything. It makes me just want to sing.

JIM: Well, let's not do that, Elizabeth. Not after all that music and stuff we had to listen to at the prom tonight. I don't think I've ever heard so much noise in one place.

ELIZABETH: Jim, why do you always have to be the old fuddy duddy? Everybody else was just laughing and talking and having the time of their lives, and you just sat there drinking your punch and talking to Ben.

JIM: First, Ben was one of the only people in the room who was not all stupid and giddy over a dumb ol' dance. I'd rather discuss football with him any day than dance with every cheap tramp in town there. Second, how do you know that was punch?

ELIZABETH: James William Parker.

JIM: Don't start that whole-name crap. You sound like my mother!

ELIZABETH: (*Begging.*) It's prom night, sweety.

JIM: And?

ELIZABETH: It's prom night. The highlight of our high school years and . . .

JIM: Elizabeth, the highlight of my high school years will be leaving that God-forsaken excuse for a school.

ELIZABETH: You never cease to amaze me.

JIM: I take that as a complement.

ELIZABETH: But no matter what, I do, um, well . . .

JIM: (*skeptical*) What?

ELIZABETH: Never mind.

JIM: What?

*Entering from stage left in 1978 is **ALICE**. **ALICE** is forty-years old. She is wearing an extra-large moo-moo. It is multicolored. She wears something, such* *as a hair decoration, that is yellow.* **ALICE** *never sees or hears* **ELIZABETH** *or* **JIM**, *and they are also completely unaware of her.*

ELIZABETH: Never mind.

JIM: No. I am very perceptive. Almost brilliant. What were you gonna say?

ELIZABETH: I wasn't "gonna" say anything, Mr. Parker.

ALICE: (*in frustration*) Why?

JIM: Did you say anything?

ELIZABETH: I said that I wasn't "gonna" say anything, mister.

JIM: No, Elizabeth. I heard that. I thought I heard someone else.

ALICE: I don't understand. Why would he do that? After twenty years! I don't understand. I don't understand.

ELIZABETH: I *was* going to tell you that, well, um. Jimmy?

JIM: What?

ELIZABETH: I'd like to be serious with you, but I can't. Everything I try to talk about, you get really sarcastic with everything and never listen to me.

JIM: Okay. Okay. Let me think. Let me focus. Okay. I'm listening.

ELIZABETH: Yes.

ALICE: (*Crying.*) Why?

ELIZABETH: In the midst of everything and all. Oh, Jimmy. I'm so nervous. I don't know how to tell you this.

JIM: (*Suddenly frightened.*) What are you talking about? I most certainly know what you **can't** say.

ALICE: No.

ELIZABETH: No.

ALICE: Not for long. This couldn't have been going on for that long.

JIM: What then? What is it, Baby?

ELIZABETH: First, is there anything you want to tell me?

JIM: Anything I want to tell you?

ELIZABETH: Anything?

*MARY, 39, runs in from stage left. She is **ALICE'S** sister and is frantic to find her. **MARY** is wearing a multi-color earth-tone blouse and mustard-colored polyester pants.*

MARY: Alice!! Alice!! Where are you?

JIM: Is there something I should say?

MARY: Alice, honey? Are you here? Are you okay?

ALICE: I'm over here.

ELIZABETH: Jim, do you realize that you could be shipped off to Vietnam? President Johnson said that the conflict is getting worse. (*JIM is silent*) You're about to graduate. You could be drafted. You could … (*She starts crying.*)

ALICE: I could just die.

MARY: Oh, Alice. (*Goes to her*) Oh, dear. It's not that bad.

*JIM goes to **ELIZABETH** and starts to comfort her.*

ALICE: Not that bad? Not that bad? Mary, Bruce just told me that he was leaving me. After twenty years! Leaving me!

MARY: I know. I know.

ALICE: That's bad.

MARY: I know.

ALICE: And he announced it in front of my family. *My* family!

MARY: (*trying to make her feel better*) He's a, a cad.

ALICE: A cad? A cad? (***Gloria** nods her head*) A cad is someone

17

who forgets to open a door for an old lady. "Cad" is not exactly the word I had in mind.

MARY: You just think it, dear. Just think it. I'd rather not actually hear it. Whatever word you come up with in your mind, I agree. Granted, as long as it's not a *profane* one. You know.

ALICE: Well, the profane is flowing in the Bruce section of my head right now, Mary.

JIM: It'll be okay, Elizabeth. I doubt if I'll get drafted. The President also said that it'll be over soon. He wants to be out by Christmas. They won't call me for that short a period of time.

ELIZABETH: Christmas of when? 1969? 1970? What if it goes on that long?

JIM: Aw, come on now. Don't be pessimistic. *(He starts to laugh)*

ELIZABETH: You're laughing?

JIM: Sorry. I just never thought I'd be telling someone else not to be pessimistic.

ELIZABETH: *(Chuckles, then in a different tone)* Jimmy, I'm scared.

ALICE: I'm scared.

JIMMY: I know.

MARY: I know.

ALICE: I can't remember not being married. It's all I've ever known.

MARY: Remember when we were little girls? Momma always used to tell us that when we grew up, we'd have to be strong and be ready to take care of ourselves if need be.

ALICE: I remember.

MARY: After Daddy died, she had to learn the hard way.

ALICE: This is different, though. My husband. My Bruce *(cries)* has been cheating on me. For over ten years. *(cries openly)*

MARY: Scum, pure scum. *(Worried about her "rough" language.)* Sorry, Alice. Didn't mean to get carried away there.

ALICE: "Scum" is okay. I think it's called for. (*pauses*) But, I, love him, Mary.

ELIZABETH: (*looking Jim in the eyes*) Are you sure you don't have something to tell me?

JIM: (*frightened*) Huh?

ALICE: I love him. I can't help it.

ELIZABETH: There's nothing you want to tell me?

ALICE: I love him. I made a vow to him. I love him.

JIM: I love you?

ELIZABETH: Is that a question or a profession?

JIM: Huh?

MARY: But he has broken that vow to you, dear.

ELIZABETH: Are you asking or telling?

JIM: Telling?

ALICE: (*cries*) I know. I just don't know what I'm going to do.

ELIZABETH: Well, say it like you're telling. It sounds like a question. (*Pauses.*) Unless, you don't mean it. Then don't say it at all.

ALICE: What?

JIM: I love you, Elizabeth Michelle Carpenter.

They both pause. All four characters freeze for just a moment.

ELIZABETH: There you go with the whole name stuff. You sound like my mother. (*She laughs.*)

JIM: That's my line.

ALICE: I've been married my whole life. Building a home. Washing, cleaning, trying, (*pauses*) hurting. Mary, I've done my best. I have loved him...with all my heart.

ELIZABETH: You love me? Really?

GLORIA: I know.

JIM: Yes.

ALICE: What am I going to do now?

MARY: (*searching*) There are, well, lots of things you could do. I mean, we're living in a modern world. It's 1978. You'll make it.

ELIZABETH: You're not just saying it to make me ecstatically happy?

JIM: (*less than convincing*) No.

ELIZABETH grabs him and hugs him tightly.

MARY: Walter and I will help. You can get a job.

JIM: Well? (*as if in anticipation*)

ALICE: My! It's been a long time.

ELIZABETH: What?

ALICE: I haven't been officially employed in over twenty years.

JIM: How do you feel about me? I mean, I've been all verbal and everything here--in a manner very unlike me--I might add. I mean, I hope you love me.

ELIZABETH: Let's get married.

MARY: Lisa's in college now. And she's on a full scholarship —everything paid. You can take care of yourself. You're strong.

JIM: Married?

ELIZABETH: Married!

JIM: We're still in high school.

ELIZABETH: For two more weeks.

JIM: Married?

ALICE·   Oh, I've got to tell Lisa. She'll be devastated.

MARY: No, she won't.

ELIZABETH: This summer. Next month.

JIM: Next month?

ELIZABETH: June. Yes, I've always wanted a June wedding.

MARY: She's never liked her father, Alice.

ELIZABETH: June. June the fourteenth. June 14, 1967. What a wonderfully sounding date for a wedding!

JIM: We're going a little fast here, aren't we?

ELIZABETH: June 14th. Wait until I tell my mother.

ALICE: Lisa loves her father.

MARY: There's a big difference between "like" and "love," honey.

ELIZABETH: Come on, let's go. I can't wait to tell everybody.

JIM: Elizabeth!

*ELIZABETH drags **JIM** off-stage.*

MARY: A lot of people really don't like Bruce. They put up with him because he's your husband.

ALICE: (*genuinely shocked*) Mary! Don't like Bruce? Are you serious?

MARY: As serious as I can be. I'm so sorry to tell you. You know how I hate to be the harbinger of bad tidings.

ALICE: I thought . . . I thought . . . I thought everybody loved him. I thought there was something wrong with . . . Mary, are you serious?

MARY: Yes.

ALICE: I thought I was just . . . just misjudging him. Mary, I love him. I really do. But, for years I have felt that . . .

MARY: I know, Alice. You've been a good wife, a good mother.

ALICE: I tried. I tried.

MARY: We all know.

ALICE: For years, I have felt that . . .

MARY: We know. We all know.

ALICE: You've known this was coming? (*MARY just looks down.*) I mean . . . I need to sit down.

MARY: Nobody knew **what** was happening. We only knew that **something** was happening. . . And . . . Alice, . . . I am so sorry. I don't know what to say. I really don't know what to say. Earnestly.

*While **MARY** is talking, an elderly woman, **STELLA**, 75, slowly walks on stage in 1986.*

STELLA: Ernest? *(She is looking around--confused--as if she is looking for someone.)* Ernest?

***STELLA** is dressed in traveling clothes. Every time we see her, she wears a hat of some sort. She is carrying a black handbag.*

MARY: I do know that you will keep survive. There are a lot of us who love you. You're gonna make it.

STELLA: Ernest? Are you listening to me?

ALICE: Thanks, Mary.

STELLA: Don't you go ignoring me again!

ALICE: Everybody's still back at the house, aren't they?

MARY: I think so. I think they're probably all still in shock. It's not everyday somebody makes an announcement like that in front of a family get-together.

STELLA: Well, I know you can hear me, Ernest. I did it. I got away. I escaped from that, that penitentiary, or old-folks home, or whatever fancy name they got for it. I walked right out the front door. Caught the nurse slave-drivers not looking and pranced my old butt right out the front. They never noticed me. Sure, by now, they probably have the state police hunting me down, but that's no matter. I can outdo them.

ALICE: I need to go home. I just don't know if I can face everybody.

MARY: Alice, honey, you have no reason don't to feel that way. We're all on your side.

ALICE: It's embarrassment, Mary. I feel like a fool.

STELLA: I have no intention of going back. They probably have a room all ready for me for my shock therapy. I know what they're up to. I know, Ernest.

MARY: You're not a fool. You've been mistreated. Mistreated, Alice.

STELLA: Ernest, you listen to me. You owe me. There's no telling what you're doing now. I don't like not being able to see you every day. I most certainly hope you are behaving.

MARY: Let's go home. Come on.

ALICE: I don't know if I can make it.

MARY: Ally, you can. I have no doubt about that.

MARY and ALICE walk off arm-in-arm.

STELLA: You've been gone for quite some time. She sits down on the bench. You've probably found you another woman. Who is she, Ernest? Mabel Consbury? Flora McGuire? Or is it Doris Crenshaw? You always liked her. I know. I know. You swore you didn't, but I have eyes. I'm not stupid, you know. She takes off her shoes. The state police? Bull! They probably have the national guard and the FBI looking for me now. You'd think I was a criminal or something. It's your daughter. She's the one who put me in the trap. A home, they call it. It's more like a cell. Trying to get rid of me. I guess I'm a constant reminder of days gone by. Past events. It's easier not to look at me. You're gone. Nobody has to remember by looking at you. But me? I just won't die. And don't get a smirk on your face. You're not innocent, Ernest. You are just as guilty as I am. I know people can't forget. I have, though. Or at least I have tried to. It does come back every once in a while. No, you don't like me discussing this, do you? You never did. Maybe we needed to? Ever think about that? Huh? Maybe we need to talk about it! Do you see where I am? Recognize this place? And don't pretend to be ignorant. You know. Remember that tree? That's where you first touched me. I knew at that moment that I had never been touched before. Just your hand on my shoulder. A simple gesture. But, my! It was twenty-five years ago. Twenty-five years. I'll never forget it as long as I live, which may make for a short memory. She laughs. I had just come to the park. I wasn't going to come, but Alan was going to be late. I was mad and depressed, so I just came here. I just watched kids play. Those were simple times. School had just started. Anna and Bruce were both in high school, doing their thing. By that time, Anna had already met Jack. You know, he turned out to be a good son-in-law. Really. But anyway, times were simple. Things were good, but I was unhappy. I guess I was selfish. I can be, you know. What made me come here that day? I don't know whether to curse or bless that day. September 10, 1961. September 10, 1961, Ernest. You touched me that day. You touched me. 6:05 in the afternoon. You just had to be there, yourself. *She stands and begins to walk around.* You're not even a park-type person. Just walking by.

WALTER, 21, enters in 1956. He is dressed in a suit with a yellow pocket handkerchief visible and carries a briefcase. As STELLA stands and begins to walk around, he sits on the bench.

STELLA: (*Continues.*) You stood there by that tree like a, like a, well, like the most handsome man I had ever seen in my life. And I was no spring chicken. I had been around the pen a few times. I'd seen quite a few specimens in my time. It's like you knew me. You just stood there, staring at me with that Clark Gable grin. You were trying to seduce me, weren't you? You knew how to pour in the charm. You were good, very good. No mention of a wife or a daughter. No talk of anything other than what I wanted to hear. Then you touched me. Ernest, how dare you. You ruined my life. *She starts to cry. Then she stops suddenly.*

WALTER: (*Looking at his watch.*) Man, oh man, is time slow!

STELLA: No, I'm not going to do this. It is just as much my fault. I did it, too. We both went into it with open eyes. A park! A park! I mean, of all places! I feel so . . . Well, so . . .But I also am glad that we ended up together. You have no idea how much I loved you. You and your wandering eye. I know. I know. "Never since I met you have I looked at another woman." Like I believe that! Ernest. This is more than I can bear. I think everybody still holds it against us, against me, anyway. The park. Why did I come here? Why did you leave me? Dead? Sure. You can hear me. I need you back here this instant. Ernest, I can't spend the rest of my life with this on my mind. Every time I see your daughter, she . . . her eyes look just like . . . Ernest, I can't do this. She hugs the trees and sobs.

WALTER: Andrew. Where **are** you? Where **are** you? Will noon ever get here?

ANDREW, 28, enters. He is also wearing a suit, a yellow tie, several rings and is carrying a piece of luggage of some sort.

ANDREW: Walter. Walter. How are you today?

WALTER: There you are!

ANDREW: I'm early, Walter. We weren't supposed to meet until noon.

WALTER: The sooner the better, though.

ANDREW: How's Mary?

WALTER: She's fine, Andrew. She's fine.

ANDREW: So, you liking married life, Mr. Newlywed?

WALTER: Well, we haven't had much time. We've only been married two weeks. It takes a lot of getting used to. We haven't even been able to move into the house yet.

ANDREW: Where are you living?

WALTER: With Mary's parents.

ANDREW: Ewww!

WALTER: It's not that bad. Well, not really bad. Seriously.

ANDREW: You're more patient than I am, Walter, my friend.

WALTER: It won't be for long. I mean, we have the deal on the house. I just need to get the down payment to them. And we got a new car yesterday.

ANDREW: Is that your car out by the gate?

WALTER: Yes.

ANDREW: Man, oh, man. Is that brand new?

WALTER: Just off the show room floor, a '56 Ford.

ANDREW: Well, Walter, the business is treating you good, isn't it? Looks like you're making some *lucrative investments*.

WALTER: Shh. Keep your voice down. The trees have ears.

ANDREW: What?

WALTER: The trees have ears.

ANDREW: That don't make no sense, Walter.

WALTER: "Doesn't make *any* sense."

ANDREW: Glad to see you agree with me.

WALTER: Andrew, do you have the money?

ANDREW: Is the sky blue?

WALTER: *(Almost to himself)* On good days.

ANDREW: Yes, sir.

ANDREW opens up the container and shows WALTER the contents.

WALTER: Wow! Is that all of it?

ANDREW: Down to the last cent.

WALTER: Yes. *(Breathes a sigh of relief.)*

ANDREW: Is that enough for your down payment?

WALTER: Plus some.

STELLA: Ernest! You'd better be listening to me.

ANDREW: Well, unless I'm horribly mistaken, this should end our business dealings for a little while, Walter.

WALTER: Yes.

ANDREW: Well, you have my phone number. I can get yours. We'll being seeing each other soon. I have a feeling, Walter.

WALTER: I don't know.

ANDREW: Maybe at the company picnic. *(Begins laughing uncontrollably as he starts to leave.)* The company picnic!

WALTER holds the piece of luggage up close to his chest and hugs it. He puts his head down. As he does so, STELLA begins walking around slowly in the background. Then, a beautiful young woman, NICOLE, 29, enters in 1999. She is wearing a dark, modern woman's business suit and wears something yellow. She holds a purse and a day planner and is talking on a cellular telephone.

NICOLE: I don't really care. No, Mother. I will not. I already discussed it with Daddy, and he let me know how he feels. I know. I am aware of that. Yes. I am. I am quite aware of that. But if it is not his choice, he wants no part of it.

WALTER: What have I done?

STELLA: What have I become?

NICOLE: I know what I'm doing.

STELLA: I don't understand.

WALTER: I'm just trying to give Mary everything she deserves. She deserves everything I can give her. And more. There's nothing wrong with that.

NICOLE: I am taking the job, Mother.

STELLA: Such a distance.

WALTER: She means the world to me.

NICOLE: It's my life.

WALTER: She's my whole life.

STELLA: My life. My life. Such a distance I've come.

NICOLE: I'll tell you what. I am coming home. We can discuss it better in person. The phone is not the best place.

WALTER: I hope I'm doing the right thing.

NICOLE: I'm in a park, Mother. Yes, a park. Benches, trees, squirrels, the whole shebang. No, I'm alone.

STELLA: I've gotta go. They'll find me.

STELLA picks up all her stuff and exits the opposite direction from which she entered.

NICOLE: I know. I love you, too, Mom, both of you. But this is the chance of a lifetime. Italy! Italy, Mother!

WALTER: May God have mercy on me.

WALTER picks up the two briefcases and exits the direction from which he entered. NICOLE sits on the bench.

NICOLE: Okay. Okay. When I get home. Want me to pick up some Chinese? (*Pauses.*) Are you sure? Yes, at the park. I just want to sit here a little while. Yes, it's safe. I promise. I'm a big girl now. I know. But it's a park, for heaven's sake, Mother. Yes, I have my stun gun. Okay. Bye. Okay. I'll be there in about an hour. Good-bye. Bye. (*She ends the call and puts her phone away. Almost immediately, she gets it back out of her purse and makes a call.*) Sharon? Yes. This is Nicole. Yes. Wait a minute. Let me talk. Yes. They offered it to me. (*Excited.*) Yes! At the full salary plus about ten percent more than I had expected! Are you crazy? Yes, I'm gonna take it. I'd be a fool not to. I know. Yeah, I have already. They're not too happy. I'm going over there tonight to get it all out in the open. Daddy will not be a happy camper, but when is he ever? Yeah. Italy. Italy! Can you believe it? Yes, the land of romance. And some of the best business opportunities on the continent. (*Grinning.*) You never know: I might find me one of those Italian hunks! You know what they say. My, oh, my! I can see them now. Yes, yes, Sharon. The money. Mula, mula, mula. They picked the best choice for the job. They call me their fighter.

*Entering from the left is **SPADE**, 24, and **VINCE**, 22. They are both wearing karate uniforms with yellow belts.*

SPADE: Look, man. I'm a lover, not a fighter.

VINCE: Oh, is that what you are? Coulda fooled me. *(Laughs out loud obnoxiously.)*

SPADE: Very funny, very funny, Vincent.

VINCE: *(visibly upset)* Hey, Spade. Don't ever call me that.

SPADE: Well, lay off the poor attempt at humor then.

VINCE: *(matter-of-factly)* Eh.

NICOLE: No, it'll be okay. Yeah. I know them. It's Spade. Yeah, Spade. That guy. I'll talk to you tonight, okay? Okay. Bye-bye. Yeah, Italy. Bye-bye. *(Ends conversation and puts phone away.)*

SPADE: Karate's just not my thing. *(They notice **Nicole**.)*

NICOLE: Spade Youngblood.

SPADE: Well, look who's here, would ya? Nicole, Nicole, Nicole.

NICOLE: Spade, Spade, Spade.

SPADE: Nicole, Nicole, Nicole.

VINCE: Who, who, who is this?

SPADE: This is Nicole Wright.

VINCE: *(Leaning to Spade and attempting to whisper.)* Notch on the belt?

SPADE slaps him on the shoulder.

SPADE: This is the sister of my best friend of my childhood. Richie Wright? Remember him?

VINCE: Ah, yeah. Richie Rich.

NICOLE: Spade, nice to see you. Most of Richie's friends I'd rather sit through a root canal than to see again. But you were never *that* bad.

SPADE: *(Thinking.)* Thanks, I think.

NICOLE: You know what I mean.

SPADE: So, what's the Rich-man doin' these days?

NICOLE: As little as possible.

VINCE: Sounds like *Rich*.

SPADE: He ain't in college no more?

NICOLE: No. No more.

SPADE: Couldn't cut it?

NICOLE: He found other talents.

VINCE: Sounds like *Rich*.

SPADE: What about you? You're dressed all fancy. What you got goin"?

NICOLE: Just business. *(Almost with a smirk)* In fact, I'm about to move to Europe.

VINCE: Cool.

SPADE: Europe, huh?

NICOLE: Europe. Teaching karate now?

SPADE: Huh?

NICOLE: Karate. The uniforms? Martial arts?

SPADE: Aw, no. This is nothing, a mistake. *(Looks at **Vince**.)* Something Vince wanted me to try. It's not me.

NICOLE: I see. Not a fighter?

VINCE: *I* like it.

SPADE: I'm not into it. Too much . . . too much . . .

NICOLE: Discipline?

VINCE: Yeah.

SPADE: No! Not discipline. I don't know what. Just not discipline.

NICOLE: I see.

SPADE: We all have our things. This just ain't mine.

NICOLE: What is?

SPADE: Huh?

NICOLE: What is yours?

SPADE: What are you? A guidance counselor?

VINCE: Cool.

NICOLE: No. Just curious.

SPADE: I work.

NICOLE: Really?

SPADE: Really.

NICOLE: As?

VINCE: *(As if waiting and wondering what **SPADE'S** answer will be)*
Well . . .

NICOLE: Well?

SPADE: Different things.

NICOLE: Different things?

SPADE: Look, I'm doin' all right.

NICOLE: I see.

SPADE: You see what?

NICOLE: Listen, fellows, the little reunion was nice, but I just don't have time to chitchat. I have some serious thinking to do.

SPADE: Wait a minute. I haven't found my place yet. I'm looking. I'm looking hard. I don't know where it is, but when I find it, I'll know. And I'll be happy. Got that?

VINCE: Yeah. Got that?

SPADE: I didn't have the world handed to me on a silver platter. Things ain't always been great, but I'll find my way. You'll see. I'll find something.

VINCE: So what if we ain't got nothing major goin' on. We'll find it someday.

NICOLE: Touching, gentlemen. Good luck. Now I need some time alone. So, good-bye. I'll see you at the video store. (*Sits down and takes out paper and pen.*)

SPADE: Nicole Richie Rich Wright girl, you just . . . You just . . . you just wait. (*Starts to leave.*) C'mon, Vince.

VINCE: (*Following*) Yeah. You just wait.

They exit.

NICOLE: (*Writing.*) To do. To do. Call Rich. Tell him to get a decent job. (*Puts paper down. Stares straight ahead.*) Italy. What an opportunity. I can't let this one pass me by. It's not everyday that something like this comes along. Man, oh, man. So what if Dad doesn't like it. It's not his choice. Mom's not happy, but she'll get over it. With the money I'll be making, I'll be able to fly them over anytime I want. I doubt if I'll be able to get Dad on an airplane, though. Maybe I can get Rich a good job. Or get him into a fine European university. If he'll try!

*An old man, **ARNOLD**, 70, enters in 1963. He is followed by his grandson, **JIM**. Yes, the same **JIM** from the opening of the play. However, **JIM** is younger, about fourteen. **ARNOLD** wears age-appropriate clothing for 1963. His dominant color should be blue. He should wear nothing yellow. **JIM** also wears age-appropriate clothing, but he should have something yellow.*

ARNOLD: This way, Jimmy. This way.

JIM: I'm coming, Grandpa.

ARNOLD: You see this park, Jimmy, my boy?

JIM: Yes, sir.

ARNOLD: This is one of the most special places in the world. This is where many important things have happened.

JIM: Here?

ARNOLD: Did you know that I proposed to your grandmother under that tree?

JIM: Really?

ARNOLD: Yes, sir. That very tree. Right after I got home from the Great War.

JIM: The Great War?

ARNOLD: World War I. That was a tough one, Jimmy. I saw many things I hope I never see again.

NICOLE: I'll have to try for him. I have an obligation.

JIM: Blood and guns and death?

ARNOLD: Just the tip of the iceberg.

JIM: Wow.

ARNOLD: It was nothing to be in awe of, Jimmy. It was hell. Living hell. I have never seen anything like it since and hope to never see anything like it again.

NICOLE: Discipline. That's why I'm here.

ARNOLD: Luck. That's why I'm here, Jimmy.

JIM: Yes, sir.

NICOLE: Yes, Sir-e!

ARNOLD: I am seventy years old today. Seventy. How old are you, boy?

JIM: Fourteen.

ARNOLD: Fourteen. I was working the fields at your age, Jimmy. Hard work. Things have changed. Seventy years. That's a long time. 1963. I never woulda thought I'd see 1963. It always seemed like an impossible time.

JIM: I understand.

ARNOLD: Do you? Do you, Jimmy?

JIM: Yes, sir. I think so.

ARNOLD: Good. This place is special. There is no telling what has happened right here. I know I've had a lot of good memories here. You know this is also the first place I ever kissed your grandmother?

JIM: Grandpa, I really don't wanna hear about that.

ARNOLD: Eh, Jimmy. It's all a part of life. You'll see. One day, you'll have memories here, too. It's just what happens. There is no telling how old these trees are.

JIM: Were they that tall when you were my age?

ARNOLD: Nearly about.

JIM: Wow.

NICOLE: It'll all work out. I have to do what is right for me. Nothing else matters.

ARNOLD: Jimmy, I have never been one to beat around the bush.

NICOLE: They'll get over it.

ARNOLD: I'm dying.

JIM: Dying?

NICOLE: The tears won't last long.

ARNOLD: And don't you go crying now. There's no need for it.

JIM: What? How are you dying?

ARNOLD: It just happens. It's part of things. We live, and then we die. I'm getting to the dying part real soon. In fact, very soon.

JIM: What's wrong?

ARNOLD: I don't want to get into it. I have a disease, and I don't have a long time left. I wanted to bring you out here and have you look at all this with different eyes. There is something about knowing that you will not see another spring or summer that makes you look at the one you're in real close. It sorta opens up a new pair of eyes you didn't know you had. I really don't think you do have them until you're about to lose your original ones.

NICOLE: They'll get over it.

She gathers her things and exits.

JIM: You see things different?

ARNOLD: Yes, Jimmy. Yes. We live this way of seeing things all distorted. I want you to learn to see right before you get in a rut of seeing things wrong. Look at this world. It is ripe with possibilities. You've got so much ahead of you, Jimmy. Everything that is important can be seen right here. Look.

JIM: How much time?

ARNOLD: Don't worry about that. Not a lot. But don't think about it. I'm gonna die. And it won't be long. In fact, I'd be happy if you'd just lean me upon against one of those old trees.

JIM: Would they let us do that?

ARNOLD: I doubt it, but it doesn't hurt to wish.

JIM: I don't know what to say.

ARNOLD: This is nothing to say. I didn't want a speech outta you. That's the last thing I wanted. I hear that enough from the "watch-this, watch-that" doctor. Pain in the . . . well. Remember this, my boy. Life is short. Death is long.

JIM: Yes, sir.

ARNOLD: Be one of those few who deserve life. It's not for everybody.

JIM: Does Grandma know?

ARNOLD: Unfortunately. And everyone in the tri-state area knows, too. In fact they probably knew before I did. If you want something told, tell your grandmother. Has a heart of gold, but she has the loosest tongue in the state.

JIM: Is that another life-lesson?

ARNOLD: One of the best ones.

JIM: Yes, sir.

ARNOLD: Heavens, Jimmy. You're a mannerly one. Where'd you learn that?

JIM: Mom.

ARNOLD: Figures. She always was full of bull. Manners? Huh?

JIM: Sir?

ARNOLD: Death, son. Death. The great equalizer. In the light of death, nothing seems quite as important any more. Absolutely nothing.

JIM: Yes, sir.

ARNOLD: Nothing.

A twenty-eight-year-younger **STELLA**, *47, and* **ALICE**, *20, enter, walking and talking in 1958. This is also a younger version of the earlier* **ALICE**.

STELLA: You can call me Stella. Mrs. Monroe is my mother-in-law.

ALICE: Thank you, Mrs. Monroe.

STELLA: Alice??

ALICE: Sorry. Stella.

JIM: How much time, Grandpa?

ARNOLD: Until what? Until I kick the bucket?

JIM: Well, I wasn't going to say that.

ARNOLD: Why not? Just say it.

JIM: Say what?

ARNOLD: "My grandpa is gonna kick the bucket."

JIM: Grandpa.

ARNOLD: Go ahead. You can say it. It's true.

STELLA: I am so glad that you and Bruce have set a date. I think he has made a fine choice. I'm sure you two will be very happy.

ALICE: I certainly hope so, Mrs. . . . . Stella. I love your son very much.

STELLA: And I'm sure he loves you, too.

ALICE: That is so nice. I'm just glad that you approve of me.

STELLA: Approve? I'm delighted.

JIM: My grandpa is going to kick the bucket.

ARNOLD: Good boy! Now say it again.

STELLA: You're just what he needs.

JIM: My grandpa is going to kick the bucket.

STELLA: Just be sure that he is what you need.

ALICE: Pardon?

ARNOLD: Louder!

STELLA: Make sure that the marriage is what you want. Don't make a mistake that you'll regret.

JIM: My grandpa is going to kick the bucket!!

ARNOLD: Thata boy. That sounded like you meant that.

STELLA: If you really love him, marriage can be wonderful. If not, it can be the biggest mistake of your life.

JIM: Yes, sir.

ALICE: Is there something that I should know, Mrs. Monroe, I mean, Stella?

ARNOLD: Let's head back to the house. I'd like to know any other illness or ailment I have before your grandmother sends a telegram to Russia.

STELLA: Nothing, dear. I just hope you are happy.

JIM: Don't you think she's going to miss you?

37

ALICE: I hope so, too.

ARNOLD: Your grandmother?

JIM: Yes, sir.

STELLA: Yes, sir! I have no doubt that you will be.

ARNOLD: I love her very much, Jimmy. Very much. And I have no doubt in the world that she loves me, too. Sure, she talks. And talks and talks and talks, but that is one of her only faults. We've been through a lot together. I don't regret any single second.

STELLA: I brought you out here, honey, to let you have a look at a special place. I know this is a popular park that has been here a long time, but to some people, to me, it is more. Did you know that my grandfather used to bring me out here when I was a girl? We used to sit and talk and talk. It wasn't that old then, but it was still beautiful.

JIM: I'll do anything I can to help her.

ARNOLD: I know you will, Jimmy. You're a good boy.

STELLA: There are times in life when things overwhelm you. You'll face those in your marriage. During those times, just step away, someplace like this, to think. It'll all come into perspective. I promise. We all need our space.

ARNOLD: You're a loyal one, Jimmy. That's the best trait a person can have. Loyalty.

ALICE: I think I see where you're coming from. I remember this park when we came into town to visit my relatives. I have spent many hours playing here, myself. It is peaceful, isn't it?

STELLA: That it is. That it is.

ARNOLD: Enough talk, my boy. Let's head home. I know your grandmother has too much food. It'll take us years to eat it all.

JIM: Yes, sir.

ARNOLD: One more time!

JIM: My grandpa is going to kick the bucket!

ARNOLD: Atta boy!

They exit.

STELLA: Don't you worry about a thing. If you are absolutely sure about it, it'll be fine. Time has a way of bringing about most things. Good and bad.

WALTER, 34, about thirteen years older than the first time we saw him, and his wife, MARY, 30, enter in 1969. He is wearing slacks and a regular button-up shirt. His shoes are extremely shiny. His attire must have something yellow in it. She is wearing a plain, pale yellow dress and dons nice jewelry.

WALTER: Are you sure you feel like walking around?

MARY: I'm pregnant, not dying.

STELLA: Life *and* death.

WALTER: Okay. I'm just trying to look out for you.

MARY: I'll be okay, Walter. It just feels so funny.

STELLA: And truth and honor win.

WALTER: Here, sit down.

She sits on the bench.

MARY: I'm fine, Walter. I'm fine.

WALTER: I know. It's just that we have waited so long. Thirteen years. And finally. It's an answer to prayers.

MARY: Walter, I'm so happy. I was beginning to lose hope.

ALICE: Bruce will be waiting. Mind if we go now?

STELLA: You go ahead, dear. I'll be right behind you.

ALICE walks off-stage. STELLA walks around looking while WALTER and MARY talk.

MARY: Don't get me wrong. I love my life. You have given me so much. We have always had plenty. Nice house. Nice cars. Everything I could ever want. But this . . . this . . . this will make everything complete.

WALTER: I know, honey. I am very proud.

MARY: I mean, there has been a void. I think this will fill it.

WALTER: I hope so.

MARY: Family. It's the most important thing in the world, right?

WALTER: Right. Ours will be. I just want you to have the very best and everything that will make you happy.

MARY: You mean that, don't you, Walter?

WALTER: Of course.

MARY: Oh, Walter, do you think that it might be possible that with the arrival of the baby, you could stay at home a bit more. I'm not complaining, Walter. I just would love for you to be at home at night.

WALTER: Mary, we've gone through all of this. I'm working. I want to provide you and now the baby everything I possibly can. I want you to have the best.

MARY: I think having you is the best I could ever want. You, more at home and more in the evenings.

STELLA leaves.

WALTER: *(A little upset with her statement)* Mary, it'll be okay. It'll be okay. Let me handle it. It'll be okay.

MARY: Walter . . .

WALTER: Now, with the baby coming, you have a lot to do, a lot to prepare for. It's just remarkable: the gift of life.

MARY: Yes.

WALTER: Names, names? Have you thought of a name yet?

MARY: Well, it is still seven months away, but . . .

WALTER: I know you, though. You have had names picked out for years.

MARY: Well . . .

WALTER: Which one? Arthur? Charles? Edward?

MARY: If it's a boy, I like "Nicolas."

WALTER: Nicolas? Hmmm. I never thought of that one. Is that new?

MARY: Sort of. But, Walter, I have a feeling, I don't know how, but I have a feeling that it is going to be a little girl. I just know it.

WALTER: A girl? Really? Well, that's fine. That's perfectly fine with me. And what name do you have for her?

MARY: Nicole.

WALTER: Nicole. I like it. Nicole. I promise to give her everything she needs, Mary. I will. You know I will. (*Emotional.*) If it costs any price, I will provide, Mary. I will provide.

MARY: I know, Walter. I know. (*She cradles his head on her shoulder.*)

ELIZABETH, 19, one year after we first saw her, runs on stage in 1968. She is wearing black. She is carrying an umbrella and acts as if it is raining heavily. It is obvious by her behavior that she is frantic.

ELIZABETH: Where is it?

Following her is JOAN, 21, her friend. She is wearing a dark-colored dress, a yellow poncho or raincoat, and a black slicker Gilligan-style hat similar to the hat worn by the Morton salt girl. She, too, is carrying an umbrella, trying to look after ELIZABETH.

JOAN: Elizabeth, please don't! It's raining. No, it's storming.

ELIZABETH: I have to find it. I have to find it.

JOAN: You're not even sure it's here.

MARY: There, there, my love.

ELIZABETH: It's here. It's here. It has to be. It has to be.

JOAN: *Elizabeth, please. Let's go back. Your mom is going to be worried sick*
                about us! Even if it were here earlier, it's surely washed away by now.
                It's been a flood.

ELIZABETH: (*Crying.*) No. It's here. I *will* find it. I'm not going back until I find
                it.

JOAN: You are so stubborn.

ELIZABETH: It has nothing to do with being stubborn. It is the most important
                thing I have in this world. Go back! Go back to safety. I'll look for it
                alone.

JOAN: I'm not leaving you out here in the storm, especially after dark. I wouldn't
                doubt a tornado coming to get you and sweeping you away to your death.

ELIZABETH: What?

JOAN: (*Realizing that she shouldn't have made that statement.*) I'm sorry,
                Elizabeth. I'm so sorry.

WALTER: A girl, huh? You think it's a girl.

MARY: I'm almost certain. I don't know how, but I am.

JOAN: I know this is so hard.

ELIZABETH: You don't know anything. You've not had your husband snatched
                right out of your hands. You've never had the news that the love of
                your life was dead, not only dead, but killed. Violently. Horribly. In
                the jungles of some country you'd never even heard of until a few
                years ago. You don't know how it feels to have the only person you
                ever cared for, someone who you've been married to less than a
                year, a *year*, ripped from you. To be told that he died bravely, not to
                worry, that the checks will come for years. The checks! I don't want
                any checks, Joan. I want Jimmy.

JOAN: I know.

ELIZABETH: No! You don't. It was perfect. He was perfect. It was here, you
                know. Here, last year that he told me that he loved me. It was so
                romantic. This very spot, Joan. Now he's gone. Gone! It was
                here. It wasn't two weeks later that he gave me that locket. It was
                his grandmother's. His grandmother's, something his grandfather

42

had given her when they got engaged. The locket, Joan. To me, that was the most important thing he ever gave me. It made me part of him, of his family, of all that he is. Was. And it's here somewhere. I know it is. We were out here today. This was the last place I remember having it. It is here. I know it. And I will find it. I have to. I feel naked without it. I have to have it hanging around my neck. That's part of him. I need him, Joan. I need him. I have to find it.

JOAN: (*Comforting her.*) Okay. Okay, Liz. Keep looking. We'll find it if we have to look all night. Come on. Before the water washes everything away.

*They resume their search. **ELIZABETH** looks weaker all the time.*

WALTER: That'll be fine. A girl. Nicole. Nicole Wright. My little princess.

MARY: *Our* little princess.

WALTER: (*Agreeing.*) Our.

*A young man, **RICH**, 16, carries a bag while he walks on stage. It is obvious that the bag is a much older version of the exact piece of luggage **ANDREW** gave **WALTER** earlier. RICH is about sixteen. This is 1991. He wears jeans and tan or neutral-colored shirt.*

MARY: She is exactly what we need. Exactly.

RICH: I need to stop.

WALTER: Exactly.

RICH: There is no telling how far I've walked already. But I don't care I'm doing the right thing. (*He sits in the ground and starts looking through his bag.*)

ELIZABETH: Where is it?!?

RICH: Where is it?

MARY: What time is it?

ELIZABETH: Where is it?!?

RICH: Oh, there it is. (*He pulls out a bottle of water.*)

WALTER: A quarter of six.

JOAN: (Despondently) *I found a quarter.*

MARY: A quarter of six? We need to go home. I need to call Mother and tell her that we decided upon a name.

ELIZABETH: *(Stops and sits on the wet ground.)* Jimmy!

WALTER: (*Standing up.*) Here, let me help you, Mrs. Wright. There we go.

MARY: Thank you, sir.

RICH: No matter how thirsty I get. Not matter how hunger pulls at my belly. No I will not return. They probably don't even realize I'm gone.

WALTER: Let's get you and Nicole home.

They exit.

RICH: Well, I don't need their attention or their pity. And I'm sure they don't need me. They have their precious Nicole. Nicole. Nicole. Nicole. I hope she chokes.

JOAN: We've got to keep looking. It's late!

ELIZABETH starts looking again. She is weakening.

RICH: Most precious, most special. Miss Perfect. Look under your noses, MaMa, PaPa. She's not as perfect as you think. Just because she was first. No. I'm not going to do this. I am NOT going to do this. I am just leaving. I'm old enough to take care of myself. I'm tired of the phonies. All of them. No more. I'm not a kid. I'm sixteen. I can get a job. I can do lots of things. I don't need their precious money. Dirty money. I don't want it.

ELIZABETH collapses. JOAN runs to her.

JOAN: Elizabeth! I've got to get you in. You're going to die of pneumonia. Come on.

ELIZABETH: (*Very weak*) The locket. Got to find the locket.

JOAN: *We'll get it. We'll find it. (*Helping her up.*) Come on. Come on, Elizabeth. Let's get out of this storm. Come on.*

ELIZABETH: The locket . . .

JOAN: I'll get it. I'll find it. I promise.

They exit.

RICH: I can make it on my own. (*Laughs.*) I wonder if Spade is going to be okay without me! Man, he needs help. *(Looks around.)* I hope this is the right decision. Oh, there's that tree I fell out of and broke my arm. PaPa was so angry at me. Hmph. What a memory. I'd relive that day again. I swear I would. I don't care about the pain. I mean, everybody was looking. Right here. PaPa looked me right the eye at the hospital. Right in the eye, and told me how stupid that was. I think that was the first time he had ever looked at me square in the eye before.

LISA, 20, ALICE's daughter, runs on stage laughing. It is 19801. She acts as if she is being chased. She is wearing a white half-blouse, white shorts, a yellow neck scarf, but no shoes.

RICH: The first time ever.

LISA: Over here, over here, Lazy Bones.

STEVE, 22, runs onto the stage laughing, too. He is a nice-looking young man. He is wearing a pair of red shorts, but nothing else. He is carrying a black-and-white shirt in his hands.

STEVE: Who are you calling lazy, Lisa? (*She laughs and begins running around.*) Huh?

LISA: You! (*Laughs.*)

STEVE: Me? Hey, I'm the one who just finished his college degree, thank you. Thank you, Miss College Sophomore.

LISA: Hey. I'm a Junior, thank you very much, Mr. Degree.

STEVE bows.

LISA: Get your shirt back on, Steve.

STEVE: Why?

LISA: Because someone might see you.

STEVE: See me?

RICH: He saw me.

STEVE: So what? (*He flexes.*) I want them to see me. I'm not ashamed of my body.

LISA: It's nice. But this is public.

STEVE: There is no one out here. Besides, it is warm weather. I like going without a shirt. Heaven and hell, let's take everything off, EVE! We could have our own little Garden of Eden.

LISA: Down boy! (*She looks around.*) But you are right. It's beautiful out here. Like an Eden.

STEVE: You mean we can walk around like Adam and Eve? (*He jokingly starts to remove his shorts.*)

LISA: Whoa! Hey. I didn't say that. (*He stops and smiles.*) It's just pretty out here. It's the first time I've been here in a long time. And for the first time in a long time, I'm happy. I really am.

STEVE: With me?

LISA: (*Pauses.*) Yes. You'll have to be patient with me, Steve. I mean I have a hard time trusting men.

STEVE: Hey, I have never . . .

LISA: I know. I know. You have never done anything to hurt me that I know of. Sure, you are a little perverted. (*He bows.*) But you have been good to me. It's just hard to forget some things. You know, my dad left my mom three years ago. They had been married twenty years. Twenty years. And he had been sneaking around for years. It nearly killed her. It did.

STEVE: She's doing well now, though.

LISA: *Yeah. She's not over it, but she's a lot stronger than she thought she was. And that's what's on my mind. Look, I won't be a fool. I have to know that a man is who he says he is. I want to know everything, warts and all. And . . . and he needs to be upfront and straight with me. If he can't devote himself to me, I don't want him. But I want to make sure before I say the*

*first "I love you." I want a one-woman man. For a lifetime. (*Silence.*)*
Did I strike you with awe or put you to sleep?

STEVE: Neither. I'm just thinking.

LISA: About?

STEVE: Our little Eden.

LISA: Okay, Steve.

STEVE: It's "Adam."

RICH: Man, I gotta get outta here before anybody finds me. Not that anyone is looking, but I need to go. (*Falls back and looks up.*) God, help me. Please. Please hear me. I need someone to hear me. Please hear me, God. *(He cries.)*

LISA: Which one holds the forbidden fruit?

STEVE: All of them.

RICH: God! Hear me.

WALTER, now fifty-six years old, enters. He is wearing age-appropriate clothing, but still has something yellow on.

WALTER: What do you think you are doing?

RICH: (*Surprised.*) Father?

WALTER: What do you think you are doing?

RICH: Uh. Just . . .

WALTER: I'm waiting.

RICH: I was just out for a while. What are you doing out here?

WALTER: Looking for you. Your mother is worried sick. She has some foolish notion that you have run away.

RICH: Looking for me?

WALTER: A suitcase, huh?

RICH: You're looking for me?

WALTER: Get that suitcase and come on, Richard.

RICH: I think I'm gonna . . .

WALTER: I think you're coming with me. There's no need in this. There is plenty for you at the house. Anything we have there is yours.

RICH: What?

WALTER: I knew you'd be here. Everything happens in this park. It's like it has a magnet in it or something. Come on, son. Let's go.

RICH: Yes, sir.

They exeunt.

LISA: We need to make sure to watch out for serpents.

STEVE: (*Looking at her.*) Do you trust me?

LISA: *Huh?*

STEVE: Do you trust me?

She stares for a long time.

LISA: Yes. Yes, I do.

STEVE: Good.

LISA: What do you want?

STEVE: Nothing. Just for you to trust me.

JIM, fifteen, enters. He is wearing a suit. It is 1964.

STEVE: I don't want anything from you. Just your trust. I promise I'll keep it in very safe keeping.

She starts to cry.

STEVE: Don't cry. Why are you crying? Did I say something wrong?

LISA: No. No. You said something right. Very right. (*She hugs him.*)

JIM: Well, Grandpa. They wouldn't let me do it. I tried. I even told the undertaker. I said, "My grandpa wanted to put away right next to that old tree in the park." They wouldn't listen, though. They said that you had to have a "proper burial" at the family plot. I've never seen so many dead people in my life. Their graves, I mean. (Pauses.) I really don't know what to say. It wasn't easy. Not at all. I didn't like seeing you up in that coffin all dressed in a stuffy suit. That wasn't you. You wouldn't have worn that to my own wedding—if I ever get married.

STEVE kisses LISA.

JIM: Continues. But it wasn't easy. I can't really say good-bye to you. You've always been there for me. I listened to every story you ever told, and I would gladly listen to every one of them again. It's not a simple thing to bury someone. And I know you know that. You buried loved ones, even your mom and dad. It was hard then, too, wasn't it? But you're right. It'll be okay. I know I will. Burial doesn't mean anything but the putting away of a body. Grandma's okay. I told her that I was going to do my best to take care of her. And I will. I promised you that. I promised you.

LISA and STEVE walk off.

JIM: If you want me to do anything else, let me know. I mean it. Drop me a note, whisper in my ear or something. Okay? Grandpa, this is not as easy as it looks. This is hard. Very hard. I don't want this part of my life to be over. I know that sounds selfish, but I don't want you out of my life. Things are going to be different. And I know. I know. You told me a thousand times in the last year. Life changes. Things are different all the time. Is that another major lesson? Well, it doesn't sink in until you feel it, until it singes your heart and melts your soul. I'll try, though. I'll try. I really don't know what I want to do with my life, Grandpa. I know you probably wondered, but why did you never ask me? I guess you didn't want to pressure me. "Things happen at their own pace for a reason." Man, oh, man. You and your quotes. I don't think I'll ever be able to forget them. I want to go to college I guess. I'll probably get married. Maybe. Probably. I'm a good catch. But she'll have to be someone special, someone who you'd approve of. (Pulls a locket out of his pocket.) Then I'll give her this. I know. I know. But Grandma gave it to me today. She said it was the most precious thing you ever gave her. I'll take care of it. I promise. I can almost feel you out here. This is where I'll remember you the most. To me, you'll always be buried under that tree. It's officially yours. I think I'll put up a monument. "This tree is dedicated to my Grandpa, Arnold Samson Parker, who kicked the bucket good and hard." (Laughs.) What a place. What a place. You were right. I promise I'll come to visit you here for the rest of my life. I promise. When I'm seventy, I'll ask to be put here, too. Good-bye, Grandpa. It's time for me to get on. I'll be back.

As JIM walks off, the music rises. Then, certain characters walk on stage without speaking or looking toward the audience. They stay in character. As each begins to leave, another enters. These characters and their sequence for this part are as follows:

JOAN (21)—*looking for the locket still—shaking his head and walking off briskly—and as if the ground is still wet.*

NICOLE (29)—*talking on the cellular phone and reading at the same time.*

MARY (31)—*walking with a child in her arms. She is wearing a pink dress with a yellow sash. Stopping, looking up, and continuing.*

ANDREW (30)—*counting money—then noticing someone offstage and going to talk with him.*

SPADE and **VINCE** (26 and 28)—*eating sandwiches—oblivious to their surroundings.*

STELLA (55)—*walking through the park—looking—visibly nervous—touched the tree—leans upon it—looks about—and scurries away. She wears dark clothing with something yellow.*

RICH (18)—*wearing a gas station attendant shirt—smiling—looks at the tree and goes on.*

WALTER (56)—*just before we saw him the last time—looking for **RICH**, his Prodigal Son.*

JIM (19) *enters wearing only army pants and boots and carrying a duffle bag—he **could** be wearing a sleeveless undershirt. It is obvious that he is about to depart for Vietnam. He sets the bag on the bench, takes out an army shirt, and puts it on—he straightens his clothes, looks around solemnly, and walks off slowly, pausing to look back—as **ELIZABETH** walks onstage.*

ELIZABETH (19)—*she is completely unaware of **JIM**--dressed in black for mourning. Goes slowly to the area where she and Jim had made marriage plans. It is obvious that she is crying. She looks, waits, and leaves.*

*As she walks off, the music softens, and **ALICE** now 50, walks on with **GEORGE**, 55, her new boyfriend in 1988. She wears an outfit still containing something yellow. He wears dark slacks, a white or light-colored shirt, and a sports jacket. He does not wear a tie. He should **not** wear yellow or red. A green article of clothing—dark-green jacket or slacks or light-green shirt—would be ideal.*

ALICE: This is it. This is the park I was telling you about George.

GEORGE: It's nice.

ALICE: It's been a long time since I was here. It seems so strange. And it seems so strange to be here with . . . well.

GEORGE: I understand.

ALICE: It's been ten years, George. And I'm doing fine. I am fine. He stole a lot from me, but I'm getting it all back. Every bit if it. And I am so happy to have you here with me. Thank you for being there for me.

***GEORGE** hugs her.*

GEORGE: It's so beautiful. I think we should think about getting married right here.

ALICE: Here? (*Thinks.*) That's an idea. (*She leans on him.*) That's a good idea. It's always been such a quiet place. Nothing ever happens here.

***ARNOLD**, looking as he did at the first of the play, enters. **ALICE** and **GEORGE** sit on the bench and appear to be talking quietly as **ARNOLD** speaks to the audience.*

ARNOLD: And so it goes. Life, death, love, marriage, kids, jobs, friends. Some times are happy. Some aren't. And there's not a one of you can tell me with any certainty what's gonna happen tomorrow. People suffer and hurt, but all in all, life isn't that bad. Yeah, I have six feet of dirt over my head, but I feel like I'm leaning against this tree, watching, breathing it all in. Trust me on this: things happen for a reason. Always do. It hurts like hell sometimes—or maybe it feels like you're floating in pure joy, but it goes together for a purpose. Different times, different memories, a giant tapestry of everything we are—woven into a beautiful piece of art in a place like this. You know, at the end of each day of holy creation, the Good Book says, "And the evening and the morning were the such-and-such day." There were six of those. The seventh day was the day of rest—if I'm not mistaken. And the Evening and the Morning were the Seventh Day.

Curtain closes.

Lowery Christopher Collins (Chris) has been an educator and writer for over thirty years. He is currently a professor of English at Panola College in Carthage, Texas. He has taught at the high school, middle school, and elementary school levels and as an English and literature instructor at the college and university level. For several years, he was a high school theatre director and a gifted education consultant. He's been honored with several teaching awards, including the Young Audiences of Northeast Texas Outstanding Service to the Profession Award and the Kennedy Center's Steven Sondheim Award for being one of the most "Inspirational Teachers" in the U.S.

He is also an award-winning playwright of over thirty scripts, a weekly newspaper columnist, a short story writer, a poet, a pianist, a vocalist, a songwriter, a recording artist with Daywind Studios, the founder and artistic director of Stagelands Theatre Company, an aspiring novelist, and a (former) choir director. He's taught a variety of classes, from rhetoric and composition to literature to acting to the Bible.

He holds a Bachelor of Arts Degree in English and History and a Master of Arts Degree in English from Stephen F. Austin State University in Texas and has served on fine arts and gifted education committees as well as on a board of governors for a small playhouse.

In addition to his interests in teaching, directing, and writing, he has a fondness for lighthouses, windmills, filmmaking, salsa, sculpture, Flannery O'Connor, travel, dominos, guacamole, social media, genetics, Maine, landscaping, pillows, gospel music, Shakespeare, marbles, YouTube, quantum physics, movies, weird jokes, maps, trees, cold rooms, and Texas.

He can be reached at mrchriscollins@hotmail.com,

on Facebook at www.facebook.com/tofferdreams,

on Twitter at "tofferdreams,"

and at his website: www.ChristopherCollinsOnline.com.

To view Christopher Collins's books and other writing, visit Ponderlake Publishing, at www.ponderlake.com.

www.ingramcontent.com/pod-product-compliance
Lightning Source LLC
Chambersburg PA
CBHW020603130626
46552CB00007B/3024